Green, Black or White:
A Voyage to Mars

Mike Ludwig

Illustrated by Haeun Sung
Edited by Katharine Worthington

ISBN: 978-1-7362371-7-5

Library of Congress Control Number: 2018955403

*Special Thanks to NASA
(National Aeronautics and Space Administration)

Mike and Henry remained friends
after Martian stopped the fight;
they often thought of his words
and tried to always be polite.

Martian returned to see
how the boys were getting along;
he hoped they had realized
that fighting was wrong.

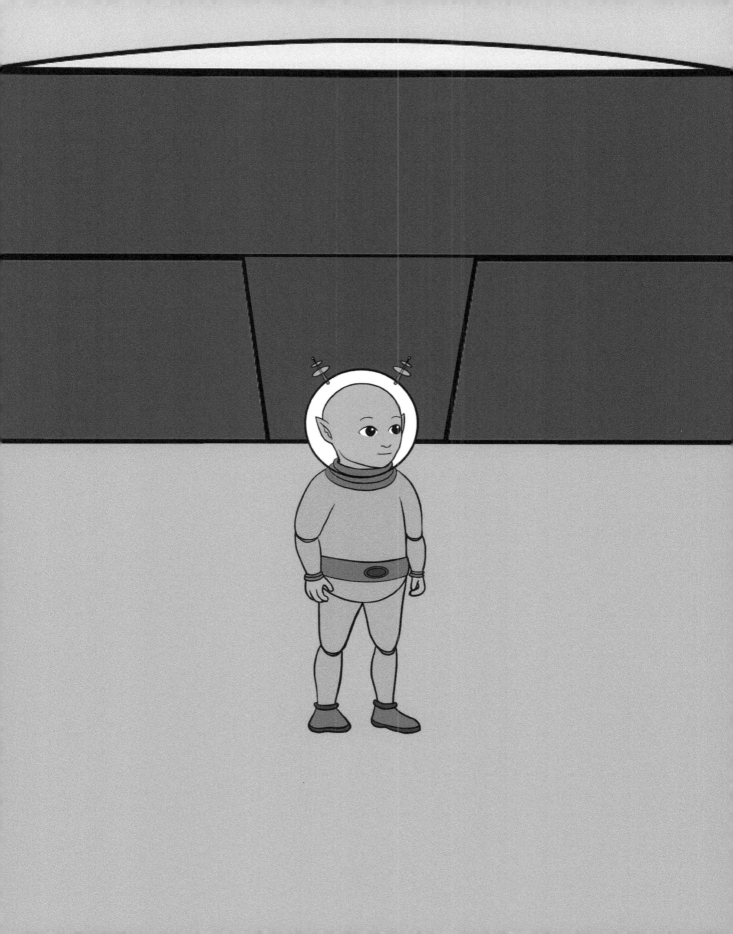

He located the school near where
the boys had started to fight.
Every student was taller than he was,
then he thought about his height.

He wondered, "I'm not as tall as them, but that shouldn't matter. Nobody should care if I am shorter, taller, thinner or fatter."

Martian found the two boys

after school in the gym;

Henry and Mike were excited

as they ran over to him.

"I returned to see
if you both were okay;
I can see that you are
by watching you play."

"We are best friends now,"

Henry replied.

"You were wise not to choose

anyone's side."

"How would you both like
to visit my planet, Mars?
We'll take my spaceship
and fly toward the stars."

Mike and Henry happily accepted
Martian's invitation.
How would they explain to their parents
this unique situation?

"We both told our parents
what happened before –
nobody could believe it.

A Martian landing on Earth
to stop a fight –
whoever could conceive it?"

"We'll still need to ask your parents
so they will not worry.
I'll promise them that you'll be safe
and we'll be home in a hurry."

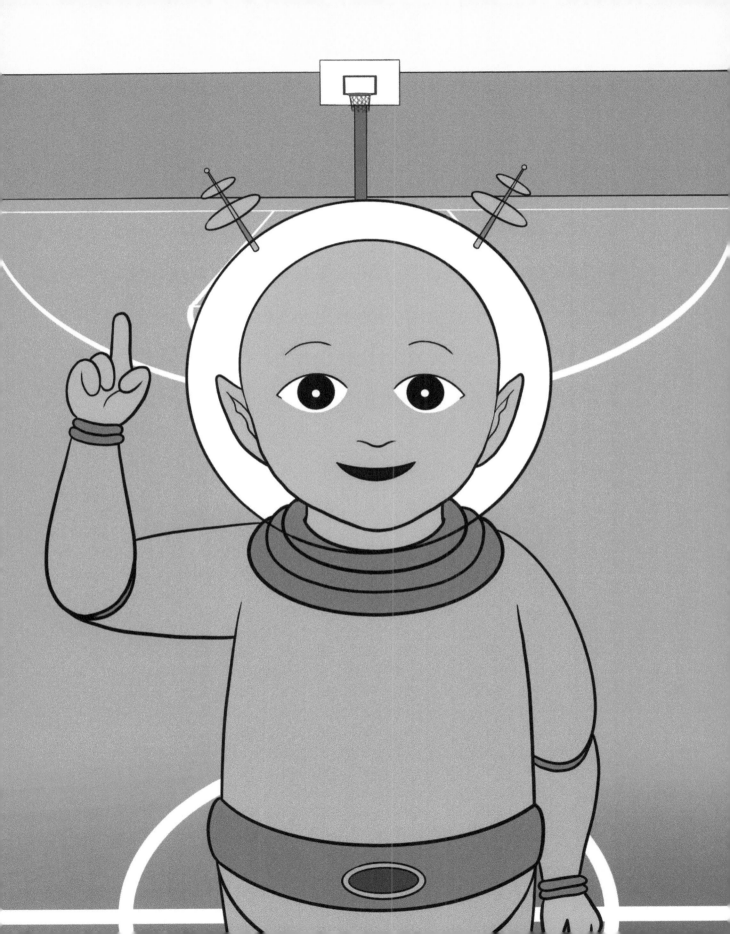

Martian agreed to meet the boys' parents,

if everyone kept it a secret.

If anyone found that out he was real,

it could be something he may regret.

Their mothers and fathers
gave them permission,
and later that day,
they were off on their mission.

The spaceship soared through the sky
with awesome power;
they arrived at Martian's planet
in only one hour.

As they landed on Mars,

Martian looked out a window.

Then he pointed to the object

that he wanted to show.

"There is the Mars Curiosity Rover
that NASA sent through the sky,
we all have to hide when
it appears nearby."

"It appears that you don't want to be seen,"

Mike replied.

"Is being afraid of our people

the reason you hide?"

"Yes, we are afraid,
but it's nothing you have done.
It's the fear of the unknown –
plus, hiding is fun!"

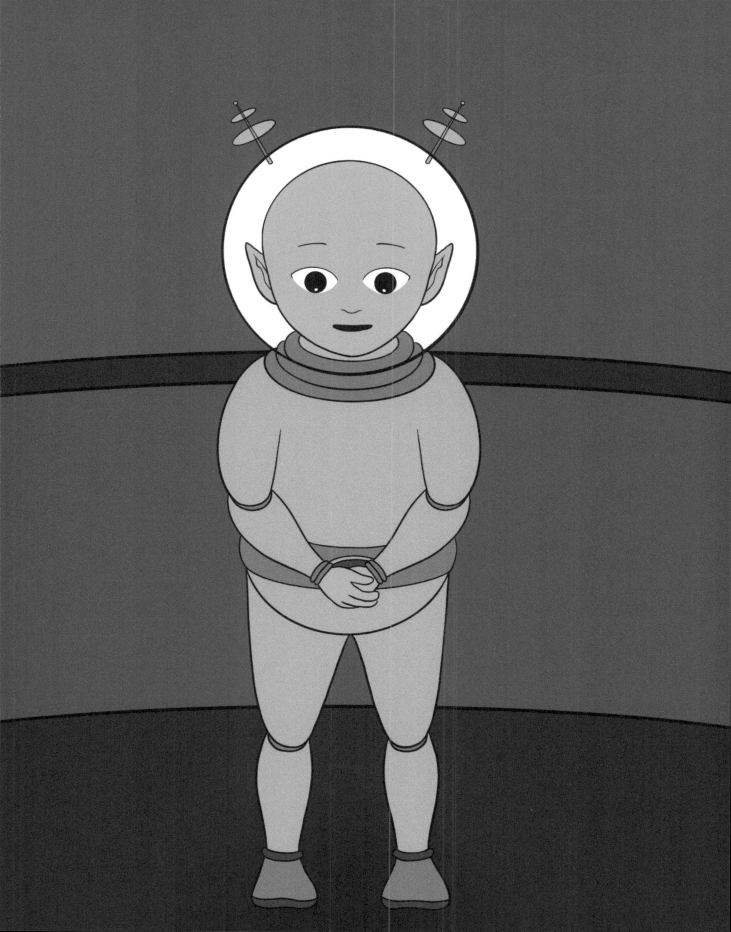

"You reminded us to be friendly,"
Henry said.
"It is okay that our planet is blue,
while your planet is red."

"You are reminding me
of what I told you,
being friendly is something
we all should do.

I hope that our leaders will

meet one day soon.

Possibly on Mars –

or maybe Earth's Moon?"

The boys noticed two Martians
out in the distance;
one waved hello as the other
started to dance.

"This is my wife, Francesca
and my daughter, Angelina.
My wife is a teacher,
and my daughter's a ballerina."

"It is very nice to meet you boys,"

Angelina said.

"You could sleep over tonight –

we have a spare bed."

"No thank you, Angelina,

it is getting late.

We promised our parents

we'd be home by eight."

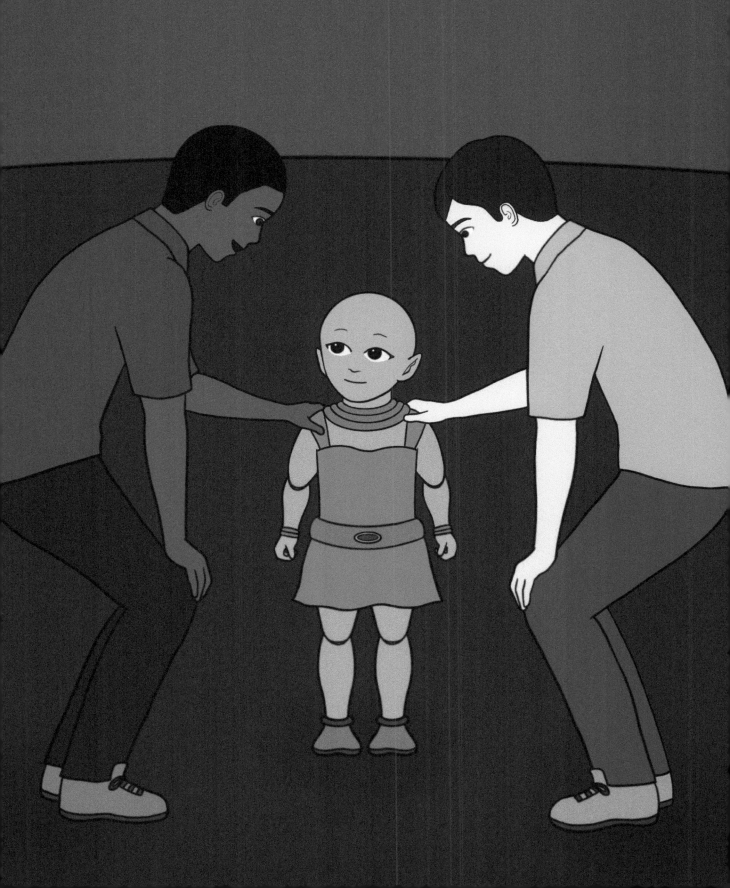

They circled Mars and its
two moons for a while;
the Martians were happy when
they saw the boys smile.

Martian piloted the spaceship

toward the boys' school.

They flew near an asteroid,

which they all thought was cool.

The spaceship landed back on planet Earth,

which from Mars appears to be a star.

The boys stared up at the sky,

amazed they had gone so far.

"We are happy that you have
seen our planet,
I doubt that you'll ever take
Earth for granted."

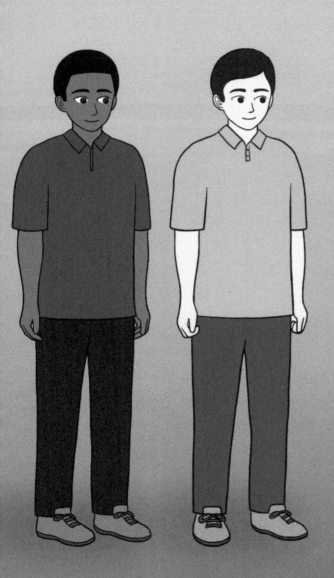

"I hope that you both enjoyed your voyage

and I'm sad this is where it ends;

Your planet Earth is beautiful –

I can't wait to tell my friends!"

The friends were sad as they
said their goodbyes.
They were all grateful,
and it showed in their eyes.

"We are happy that you have remained friends
and hope you have a good night.
You are now part of our family –
Green, Black *and* White."

Lightning Source UK Ltd.
Milton Keynes UK
UKHW051207121220
374981UK00002B/207